C000050325

Little Women

Louisa May Alcott

Simplified by D K Swan
and Michael West
Illustrated by Shirley Tourret

LONGMAN

Addison Wesley Longman Limited,
Edinburgh Gate, Harlow,
Essex CM20 2JE, England
and Associated Companies throughout the world.

This simplified edition © Longman Group UK Limited 1987

First published 1987
This impression Penguin Books 1999

ISBN 0-582-54162-X

Set in 10/13 point Linotron 202 Versailles
Printed in China.
GCC/15

This edition is based on Louisa May Alcott's
Little Women and *Good Wives*

Acknowledgements

The cover background is a wallpaper design called NUAGE,
courtesy of Osborne and Little plc.

Stage 4: 1800 word vocabulary

Please look under *New words* at the back of this book
for explanations of words outside this stage.

Contents

Introduction

Louisa May Alcott

Louisa, the second of Bronson Alcott's four daughters, was born in 1832. Her father was well known as one of the leaders of the American "transcendentalist" movement. His special interest was in the improvement of education. He had very many ideas about equal treatment for everybody in schools, and about the end of slavery and the rights of women. He was ahead of his time, and therefore many of his ideas failed, and his family was always poor until the success of Louisa May Alcott as a writer. In fact, the experiences of the four March girls in *Little Women* are very much like the experiences of Louisa and her sisters.

Bronson Alcott firmly believed that we must "trust the intelligence of children" in educating them. One proof of the truth of this belief, which is still respected by American educationists, was in the education of Louisa herself. She had a great love of books. When the family moved to Concord, one of their neighbours was the famous poet and transcendentalist writer Ralph Waldo Emerson. He liked Louisa Alcott and allowed her to use his library with its many books. She spent as much time as she could there, but she had to work to help her family. She worked as a servant, as a dressmaker, and as a teacher. All the time, she wrote.

At last, in 1852, a magazine printed – and paid for – one of her stories. Her stories for children, and especially her fairy stories, were well liked, and she became a regular writer for the magazine *Atlantic Monthly*. During the American Civil War (1861–65) she worked as a nurse in Washington D.C., and her letters from the hospital, with their very touching descriptions of wounded soldiers and their problems, had more and more readers. The letters were collected and printed as a book, *Hospital Sketches*, in 1863, and Louisa May Alcott became famous.

Little Women appeared in 1868. The literary magazines treated it as learned literature, and they disliked it. The critics in magazine after magazine attacked it. The book was too sentimental, they said, meaning that it appealed to the readers' feelings instead of exercising their minds. But the readers themselves, mainly girls and young women, were happy to have their tender feelings moved. The book was bought in very large numbers, and readers watched the bookshops and libraries for the next book by Louisa May Alcott. The story of the March girls (the "Little Women") was continued in *Good Wives, Little Men, Jo's Boys* and *Aunt Jo's Scrap Bag*. Other books poured from Louisa's pen, and she became an extremely successful writer.

All through her life, Louisa worked hard for an end to slavery in America. In her later years, as a famous writer, she gave strong support to movements in favour of women's rights and against the misuse of strong drink. Towards the end of her life, she was often ill, but she continued to write until her death in 1888.

Little Women
We have suggested that the most eager readers of *Little Women* were girls. They were not the only readers, but it is rather important to consider what provision there was for young people's reading.

Before 1868, when *Little Women* appeared, there were indeed certain books written especially for children and young people. Because of the religious (Puritan) teaching of the early American settlers and the beliefs of writers like Rousseau (his *Emile* had a strong effect on educational thinking), nearly all these books were written to teach, and especially to teach good thought and behaviour. There was not much to satisfy young people's thirst for stories (about action and real people) to exercise the imagination. For these, before the year 1800, young people had to go to books that had been written for the general reader: books like *The Pilgrim's Progress* (1678), *Robinson Crusoe* (1719), *Gulliver's Travels* (1726). After 1800, fairy stories began to appear for young children: Grimms' *Fairy Tales* (1823 in English), and the fairy stories of Hans Andersen (1846 in English).

Older children loved Washington Irving's *Legend of Sleepy Hollow* and *Rip Van Winkle* (1819). These were not written for children, but they offered young people the chance to see action in the imagination and to enjoy wondering what would happen next. And that is what Louisa May Alcott offered her readers: the characters seemed real; the readers could put themselves in the place of (identify with) one of them and share his or her thoughts and feelings.

The March sisters in *Little Women* are separate people, each with her own way of thinking. This was perhaps unusual at the time, more than a hundred years ago. In most middle-class families the girls had to be good and obey their parents, not to show independent character. Needlework and reading were all right, but you did not find a young lady brushing a path through the snow, or throwing snow at a boy's window.

Chapter 1
The four sisters

It was near Christmas-time. Four girls sat by a warm fire. They looked through the window at the snow falling outside.

"Christmas won't be Christmas without any presents," said Jo.

"Being poor makes one so unhappy!" said Meg, looking down at her old dress.

"I don't think it's fair that some girls should have pretty things and we should not," said Amy.

"We've got father and mother ..." began Beth.

"We haven't got father, and we shan't have him for a long time," answered Jo.

These four sisters, who did not like being poor, lived in the town of Concord in the United States of America. At this time there was a war between the North and the South, and their father was away with the Army, helping to take care of the sick and wounded. He had once been rich but had lost most of his money in trying to help a friend.

Meg, the eldest, could remember when there was plenty of money for everything that was needed. She was now sixteen years old and very pretty, with light brown hair, large eyes, small hands and feet. Her fifteen-year-old sister, Jo, was tall, thin and not very graceful. Jo had grey eyes and very lovely red-brown hair. She always wished she was a boy, so she did not care how she looked. She loved to run and climb trees, and do things that boys like doing.

Beth was thirteen years old, bright-eyed, with a face

1

like a rose. She was gentle and thoughtful, but was very shy, afraid of talking to people she did not know. In this she was very unlike her youngest sister, Amy. Amy was only twelve years old, but she thought that she was an important person and she was very proud of her golden hair, her white skin and blue eyes.

The girls' mother, Mrs March, was giving all her time to working for the soldiers, making them warm clothes; and the girls had given up their Christmas presents for the soldiers. That was why Jo said: "Christmas won't be Christmas without any presents."

"Mother will be coming soon," said Beth.

She put her mother's shoes to warm in front of the fire; then Jo held them up close to it so as to warm them quickly.

"These shoes are quite worn out," she said. "Mother must have new ones."

It was Christmas morning. The girls dressed quickly and went down to the sitting room. There they met Hannah, the old servant who had lived with the family since Meg was born. Hannah was loved by them all, more as a friend than a servant.

"Where is Mother?" asked Meg.

"Someone came to call her to help a family who have no food," said Hannah.

"Oh well," said Meg, "you bring our breakfast and she will soon be back."

By the time Hannah had finished cooking, the girls were very hungry. Just at that minute their mother came in.

"Happy Christmas!" they said.

Jo and Beth warm their mother's shoes in front of the fire

"Happy Christmas, my daughters," said Mrs March. "Before we sit down, I want to tell you that I have just been to a house where there are six children. Their mother – Mrs Hummel – has no fire to keep them warm and no food to give them. Hannah and I will take them some wood. Will you come with us and take them your breakfasts?"

They were all silent for a moment. Then Jo said, "What a good thing we hadn't begun to eat!"

"May I go and help carry the things to the poor little children?" asked Beth eagerly.

"I'll take the hot cakes," said Amy, bravely giving up the food she most liked.

Meg was already putting the bread and butter into a basket.

"I thought you would do it," said Mrs March, smiling. "You shall all go and help me, and when we come back we will have bread and milk for breakfast."

In the evening they acted a play which Jo had written, and a few friends came in to see it.

The play went well: the actors made a great deal of noise, and their friends shouted and laughed. Just as it was ending, Hannah came into the room and said, "Mrs March wants you all to come down and eat something."

This was not expected, even by the actors, and when they saw the table, they looked at one another with delighted surprise. There were cakes of all sorts; there was fruit, and sweets. It was a wonderful supper. In the middle of the table there was a pot of beautiful flowers.

"Where did it come from?" they all wanted to know.

"Did the fairies bring it?" asked Amy.

"Father Christmas brought it," said Beth.

"Mother did it," said Meg.

"Aunt March felt good for once, and sent us these things," said Jo.

"You are all wrong. Old Mr Laurence in the big house next door sent it," replied Mrs March.

"The Laurence boy's grandfather!" said Meg. "Why did he do that? We don't know him."

"Hannah told one of his servants that you took your breakfast to the poor children. He is rather a strange old gentleman, but that pleased him. He knew my father many years ago, and this afternoon he sent me a friendly note: 'I have heard what your children did this morning,' he wrote, 'and I am sending a little Christmas present to them.' So you have this nice meal to make up for a breakfast of bread and milk."

Chapter 2
Meg and Jo

The week after Christmas was a free time for the four sisters, especially for Meg and Jo, who had each found some work to do when their father lost his money. Meg went every day to teach Mrs King's four little girls. She did not like this work, but she did it as well as she could, because she wished to help her family. Jo spent each day with her father's rich aunt – a difficult old lady who lived in a large house nearby. Jo made herself useful by doing any of the things her aunt wanted – looking after her dog and her bird, helping to clean things and reading to her aunt.

Beth was at home all the time, helping Hannah. Before her father went away she did her lessons with him, but now she did them by herself. Mrs March had tried to send her to school, but she was too shy to learn among a lot of other children. She loved music, and she prayed for a new piano instead of the old one in which many of the notes did not sound. Amy played a little, but she was proudest of her drawing, and she wanted to be a famous painter.

One day, Meg was looking for Jo. She found her in the little room at the top of the house which was used for storing things they did not want. Jo was lying on an old bed, reading and eating apples, while a friendly mouse came to sit beside her. Meg came in with a letter.

"Such fun!" she said. "Sallie Gardiner's mother has asked us to a little dance tomorrow, and Mother says that we may go. Now, what *shall* we wear?"

"What's the use of asking that, when you know that we have only one dress each that we can wear?" said Jo.

Chapter 3
The Laurence boy

On the next afternoon the sisters began to get ready for the dance, and at last, with the help of Beth and Amy, they were ready.

As soon as they arrived, Meg began to enjoy herself. Her friend Sallie looked after her, and several young men asked her to dance. Meg danced beautifully, even though her pretty shoes hurt her. She was proud of her small feet, and sometimes she bought shoes that were not big enough.

Jo sat quietly looking across at some boys who were laughing and talking about skating. She loved skating. Jo generally liked talking to boys better than to girls, but she knew that she must not go over to join them. When a young man came towards her to ask her to dance, Jo went behind the door to escape. To her surprise she found a boy in the passage.

"I didn't expect to find anyone here," she said, preparing to go out again as quickly as she came in.

But the boy laughed and said pleasantly, "Don't go."

"Don't you mind?"

"Not a bit. I only came out here because I don't know many people, and I felt rather strange at first, you know."

"So did I. Don't go away, please, unless you'd rather."

The boy sat down again. He sat silent, looking at his shoes. At last, trying to be pleasant and easy, Jo said, "I think I've seen you before. You live near us, don't you?"

"Next door," and he looked up and laughed.

Jo laughed too, and said, "We did have such a good time with your nice Christmas present."

"My grandfather sent it."

"But you told him to, didn't you, Mr Laurence?"

"What makes you think that, Miss March?"

"I'm not Miss March. I'm only Jo."

"And I'm not Mr Laurence. I'm only Laurie."

"Laurie Laurence – what a strange name!"

"My first name is Theodore, but I don't like it."

"I hate my name too – Josephine."

They watched the dancing for a few minutes, and then Laurie said: "Don't you like dancing?"

"I like it well enough, if there's plenty of room. In a place like this I'm sure to step on people's feet, or do something wrong, so I keep out of it. Don't you dance?"

"Sometimes, but I've been away so long – at school in Italy and Switzerland and in Paris – that I don't know how things are done here."

Jo decided that she liked Laurie very much. She wondered how old he was, but did not like to ask.

"I suppose you will be going to college soon," she said. "I often see you working at your books."

"Not for a year or two," he replied. "I won't go before I'm seventeen."

"Aren't you seventeen yet?" asked Jo, looking at the tall lad who she thought must be seventeen already.

"Sixteen next month." And then, as the music began again, he said suddenly, "This is a lovely dance; won't you dance it with me?"

"I can't. I told Meg I wouldn't, because ..." There Jo stopped for a moment. But she decided to go on. "You see, the back of my dress is burnt and, although I put a piece in, it doesn't look very good. Meg told me to keep still, so that no one would see it. You may laugh if you want to; it is funny, I know."

But Laurie didn't laugh. He said very gently, "Never mind that. There is a long hall outside there, where we can dance with no one to see us. Please come."

How they enjoyed that dance together! When the music stopped, they sat down to get cool. They were just beginning to have a pleasant talk when someone came to tell Jo that Meg wished to see her. She had hurt her foot and was resting in a side room. Jo was sorry to leave Laurie, but she went at once.

She found Meg resting, with her feet on a cushion.

"I've hurt my foot," she said. "It turned over – I suppose because these shoes are too small. It hurts so much that I won't be able to walk home, but Hannah will be here soon. You go and have something to eat and bring me some coffee."

Jo got the coffee, but as she turned to carry it back she poured it down the front of her dress.

"Oh! Oh! Oh!" she cried. "Now I've spoilt my dress!"

"Can I help you?" said a friendly voice. It was Laurie. He was carrying cakes in one hand and a cup of coffee in the other.

"I was trying to get something for Meg."

"And I was looking for someone to give this to."

Jo led him to Meg. Laurie brought more coffee and cakes for Jo and they sat down together. They were so happy that Meg forgot about her foot. When Hannah came, she stood up quickly, but she soon sat down again in great pain. Laurie saw at once that she could not walk home.

"My grandfather's carriage has just come," he said. "Let me take you home in it."

"But are you going so early?" said Jo. "You don't want

Jo spills her coffee on her dress at the dance

to go home yet!"

"Yes, I do. I always go early. Please let me take you all
home."

Soon   they   were   all   on   their   way   home   in
Mr Laurence's large carriage. They said "good night" to
Laurie with many thanks, and went in quietly, hoping not
to wake their young sisters. But soon two little voices cried
out:

"Tell us about the dance! Tell us about the dance!"

Chapter 4
Visit to Laurie

One afternoon Jo came back early from Aunt March because it had been snowing heavily. She did not feel like sitting by the fire, so she took a brush and began to make a path through the snow so that Beth could walk through the garden. She watched old Mr Laurence drive away from the house next door; and then, as she was brushing away the snow near the wall which separated the two houses, she saw an unhappy-looking Laurie through one of the windows.

"Poor Laurie," thought Jo, "he's all alone. He needs a lot of friends to make him happy."

She threw a handful of snow against the window, and Laurie turned. At once his face changed. He laughed, opened the window and called to her.

She shook her brush at him as she called out, "Are you ill?"

Laurie opened the window and said in a thick voice, "I've had a cold, and have been in my bedroom for a week, but I'm better now."

"What do you find to do?"

"Nothing! Grandfather reads to me, but I don't like the books he reads."

"Why don't you get someone to come up?"

"I don't know anyone. Won't you come?"

"I will if Mother will let me. I'll go and ask her. Shut that window, and wait till I come."

Jo came back in a few minutes.

"Mother sent you her love," she said when she reached Laurie's room, "and Meg sent you this cake for your tea."

"How kind you all are!" said Laurie.

"Shall I read to you?" asked Jo.

"No, I'd much rather you talked. Tell me about your sisters. Beth is the one who stays at home, isn't she, and Meg is the pretty one, and Amy is the little girl?"

"How did you know?" Jo asked.

"Well," said Laurie, "I often hear you calling each other, and you always seem to be having such fun. I know that it isn't right to look through people's windows, but sometimes it is like looking at a picture. I see you all in the firelight, sitting round the table with your mother. I haven't any mother, you know."

He looked so sad that Jo said, "You may look as much as you like. But why don't you come and see us? Wouldn't your grandfather allow you?"

"He would if your mother asked me. He lives very much with his books. My teacher, Mr Brooke, doesn't live here in the house, so I haven't anyone to go out with, and I stay at home most of the time."

"That's bad for you," said Jo. "You ought to go out more."

"Do you like your school?" asked Laurie.

"I don't go to school. I go to look after my difficult old aunt."

Jo talked about her aunt's fat little dog and the books which she had to read to her aunt, and she made Laurie laugh till the tears ran down his face.

Then they began talking of books.

"If you like them so much," said Laurie, "go down and see ours. Grandfather is out, so you needn't be afraid."

"I'm not afraid of anything."

"I don't believe you are," said Laurie. He was afraid sometimes. He was rather afraid of his solemn old grandfather. He took Jo down to a large room filled with books and pictures. Jo looked round the room: "What a lot of books!" she said. Just at that moment the bell rang and one of the servants came in and said, "The doctor has come to see Laurie."

"Do you mind if I leave you for a few minutes?" he said.

"Of course not. I'm so happy with all these things to look at."

Jo stood for some time looking at a fine picture of old Mr Laurence. When the door opened, she said, "I'm sure I shouldn't be afraid of him, Laurie. He has kind eyes, even if his mouth is hard. Of course he's not as good-looking as my grandfather but I like him."

"Thank you, madam," said a deep voice. Jo turned quickly and saw – not Laurie – but old Mr Laurence himself.

For a minute she thought she must run away, but then she saw that he was smiling.

"So you're not afraid of me," he said.

"Not much, sir."

"And I am not so good-looking as your mother's father?"

"Not quite, sir."

"But you like me?"

"Yes, I do, sir," said Jo.

That answer pleased the old gentleman. He laughed, shook hands with her and said: "You are brave, like your grandfather, my dear. What have you been doing to my grandson?"

"Only trying to be good neighbours. He is all alone, and we girls would like to help him if we can, because we haven't forgotten your Christmas present."

Mr Laurence hears Jo talking about his picture

"How are the poor little children you gave your breakfast to?"

"The Hummels? They are doing well, sir."

"Tell your mother I'll come over to see her soon. And now let us go in to tea."

At this minute Laurie came running in. He was very surprised to see Jo and his grandfather talking together, and the old man was equally surprised, during tea, to hear Laurie and Jo talking like two old friends.

"How happy he is!" he thought. "She has done him good already."

Chapter 5
Beth gets her wish

After Jo's visit, a new life began for Laurie. Mrs March was glad to see him whenever he wished to come to the house, and soon he and the four girls were the greatest friends. Laurie spent less time on his lessons, but old Mr Laurence was pleased to see him happy in the company of people of his own age.

Meg liked wandering over the large house. Jo liked to sit for hours in the big room reading, and Amy looked at the pictures. Only Beth was too afraid to enter the house. She wanted to play the big piano, but she feared old Mr Laurence too much to go near him.

When Mr Laurence discovered this, he tried to make it easy for Beth to come. One day, when he was visiting Mrs March and the four girls, he began to talk about music and musicians. The music-loving Beth came nearer and nearer to his chair to listen.

"Laurie hasn't much time for his music now," he said, and then, as though the thought had just come to him, he went on, "I am glad because I didn't want him to spend so much time on it, but the piano should be used. I do wish that some of your girls would come and play on it sometimes. They needn't see anyone, and they won't trouble me. I'll be in my room at the other end of the house."

As he got up to go, he said, "Of course, if they don't want to come ..."

Here Beth said, "Oh, sir, I do want to."

"Are you the musical girl?"

"I'm Beth, and I do love music. I'll come, if you're sure no one will hear me."

"No one, my dear. Come as often as you like." He held out his hand, and Beth, no longer afraid, put her small hand trustfully in his, for she had no words to thank him for his kindness.

Early next morning, Beth watched old Mr Laurence go out and then she set off for the big house. After twice turning back in fear, she at last went in by a side door and made her way as quietly as she could to the room where the piano was. Laurie had left some easy but very pretty music for her, and she spent a wonderful morning playing it. She forgot her fears, herself, and everything else except the pleasure that the music gave her.

After that, Beth went to play on the piano every morning. She never met anyone, and she never knew that old Mr Laurence often sat in his study listening to her, and thinking of his dearly-loved little granddaughter who died long ago. Beth was so happy and so thankful that she decided to make some slippers for old Mr Laurence. With the help of her mother and sisters over the difficult parts, she soon finished them and sent them to him. For two days there was no reply. Beth was afraid that the old gentleman was not pleased with them. Then, one morning, when she returned from a walk, several joyful voices called out to her: "Here's a letter for you, Beth. Come quick, and read it!"

As Beth hurried in, Jo cried out, "Oh, Beth, look at what he has sent you!" They were all pointing and saying, "Look there! Look there!"

Beth did look, and turned white with delight, for she saw a small piano, with a letter lying on it for "Miss Elizabeth March". Beth opened and read it. It was a rather solemn letter, as if written to someone grown-up:

Miss March.
Dear Madam,
    I have never had any slippers which pleased me so
well as yours. I should like to return your kindness, and
so I am sending you the small piano which was once
used by my granddaughter.
    With many thanks and best wishes.
                    I am, Your friend,
                    James Laurence

All the girls gathered round to see the beautiful piano, while Beth sat down to try it. She found it perfect.

"Now you'll have to go and thank him," said Jo – half in fun, for she did not think that Beth would be brave enough.

"I am going now," said Beth, "before I get afraid."

Old Mr Laurence looked very surprised to see her.

"I came to thank you, sir." she began. But she did not finish what she was saying, for he looked so friendly, and smiled so kindly at her, that she put both her arms round his neck and kissed him.

The old gentleman was pleased by the trusting little girl. He took her on his knee, and Beth was soon talking to him as if she had known him all her life. When she went home he walked with her to her own gate, shook hands, and lifted his hat.

When the girls saw this happen, Jo began to dance with joy, Amy nearly fell out of the window in her surprise, and Meg said, "Well, I do believe the world is coming to an end."

Chapter 6
Dreamland

One fine September day, the four sisters had walked to the shaded part of a hill not far from their house. Laurie, who had been very lazy that morning, found them all working under the trees. Meg was doing needlework, Amy was drawing, Beth was gathering pretty-coloured seeds, and Jo was reading from a book to the others.

They were all so busy that they did not notice Laurie until he was quite near. Then he said, "May I join you, please – or shall I be a trouble to you?"

"Of course," said Jo. "We should have asked you before, but we thought you wouldn't want to join such a party of girls."

"I always like your parties, but if anyone doesn't want me, I'll go away."

"You can stay if you do something," said Meg. "It's against the rules to be lazy here."

"I'll do anything you like if you let me stay. I'm so tired of being alone in the house."

"Then take this book and read to us," said Jo.

Laurie took the book and read it aloud to the end. Then he said: "And now may I ask what this new plan is that you seem to have started?"

"Shall we tell him?" Meg asked, looking at her sisters.

"Well," said Jo, "we each decided to do a certain amount of work every day. Mother likes us to be out of doors as much as possible, so we bring our work here and have very happy times. We've been pretending that we are pilgrims, and that dreamland is there, over the hill."

Jo pointed, and Laurie looked through an opening in

the wood, across the fields on the other side of the river, to the green hills in the distance which rose to meet the sky. The sun was low, and the clouds were shining in the golden light, like the walls of some wonderful city.

"Wouldn't it be fun if all our dreams came true, and we could live in them?" said Jo.

"I have dreamed so many that it would be hard to say which one I'd most like to come true," said Laurie.

"Well, you'll have to decide," said Meg. "Now tell us which of your dreams you like best."

"I'll tell mine if you will all tell yours."

"Yes," said the girls, "we will. Now, Laurie."

"After I'd seen as much of the world as I wanted to," said Laurie, "I would go to live in Germany, and have as much music as I wanted, and at last become a famous musician myself. I would never trouble about money or business, but I would just live for what I like. That's my dream. Now, what's yours, Meg?"

Meg took a long time before she said slowly, "I should like a lovely house, full of lovely things, nice food, pretty clothes, plenty of money, pleasant people ..."

"Wouldn't there be a man in your house?" asked Laurie.

"I said 'pleasant people'," said Meg, not looking at him.

"Why don't you say you'd like a good-looking, wise husband," said Jo, "and some dear little children? You know that your dream house wouldn't be perfect without them."

"Well, *you* would have nothing but pens and paper and books in yours," replied Meg hotly.

"Of course. I should have rooms filled with books, and a pen which would help me to write books of my own – to make me the most famous writer in the world."

Laurie finds the girls sitting under the trees

"My dream is just to stay safe at home with Mother and Father, and help to take care of the family," said Beth.

"No other wishes?" asked Laurie.

"Not since I have had my little piano."

"I have very many wishes," said Amy, "but my favourite is to go to Rome, paint pictures, and be the greatest artist in the world."

"Oh!" said Laurie. "We all want to be rich and famous except Beth."

"I wonder where we shall all be in ten years' time," said Jo.

"I hope I shall have done something to be proud of by then," said Laurie, "but I'm almost afraid I'm too lazy, Jo."

"Mother says you'll work when you have some good reason to make you work."

"Does she? I hope she's right. I ought to work to please Grandfather, but he wants me to go to college for four years, and then be a merchant and look after his ships. But I don't want that sort of life – I should hate it. If I go to college for four years, that ought to be enough for Grandfather. If there was anyone else to stay with him, I'd run away at once to Germany and my music."

"You ought to do as your grandfather wants, Laurie," said Jo. "If he sees that you work hard now and at college, I am sure he will be kind to you. There will be no one to stay with him if you go away."

That night, when Beth played to his grandfather the simple music that the old man loved, Laurie stood outside in the shadow, and listened. He said to himself, "How lonely Grandfather would be if I went away! I'll let my dream go, and I'll stay with him while he needs me."

Chapter 7
The telegram

"November is the most unpleasant month in the whole year," said Meg, standing at the window one grey afternoon, looking out at the frozen garden.

"You *are* sad, poor dear!" cried Jo. "And I'm not surprised. You see other girls having a lovely time, while you do nothing but work, work, every day."

Beth, who was also looking out of the window, said, smiling, "Two pleasant things are going to happen: Mother is coming down the street, and Laurie is coming through the garden as if he had something nice to tell us."

Mrs March and Laurie came in together. A few minutes later there was a ring at the front door, and Hannah came in with a letter.

"It's one of those nasty telegrams," said Hannah, as if she was afraid that it would explode in her hand.

Mrs March turned white as she took it, and when she had read it she fell back, with a cry, in her chair.

Jo took up the telegram and read:

Mrs March,
Your husband is very ill. Come at once.
                    S. Hale,
          Blank Hospital, Washington.

For a moment everyone was silent. Then Mrs March said, "I'll go at once, but it may be too late. Oh, children, children, help me to bear it!"

The girls gathered round their mother as she held out her arms to them. For a few minutes, they all wept, but then Hannah cried her tears and said, "I won't waste any more time crying. I'll go and get your things ready for your journey."

"She's right. There is no time for tears now," said Mrs March. "Stop crying and let me think over my plans. Where is Laurie?"

"I'm here," said Laurie. "What can I do to help?"

"Send a telegram to say that I will come by the morning train."

"I'll go at once," said Laurie. "Is there anything else I can do?"

"You can leave a note for Aunt March. Jo, bring me a pen and some paper."

Jo knew that her mother was writing to Aunt March to ask for money for the journey. "How I wish," she thought, "that I had some money to give her."

"Now, Laurie," said Mrs March, "here is the letter. You needn't hurry because I can't travel until tomorrow morning. Jo, go and buy these things I shall need for your father. Beth, go to Mr Laurence and tell him what is happening. Meg, come and help me find my clothes for the journey."

For a time they were all too busy even to cry. Then Meg asked her mother to rest while she made her some tea. As she was doing this, old Mr Laurence came back with Beth.

"Beth has just told me about your husband's illness; it is very sad news," he said. "I have brought these things which may perhaps be useful. You may be sure that, while you are away, I shall do all that I can to help the girls. But do you feel able to go on this long journey alone? Would you allow me to come with you?"

Mrs March looked for a moment as if she would be glad for him to come. She *was* rather afraid of the long journey alone. But she soon decided that she could not allow the old man to go so far. She told him so, with the warmest thanks for his offer. He smiled and walked away, saying that he would be back soon.

Meg was bringing a cup of tea to her mother when she was surprised to meet Mr Brooke.

"I have heard the sad news of your father's illness, Miss March," he said in a kind and quiet voice, which sounded very pleasant to Meg. "I am going to Washington for Mr Laurence," he went on, "to buy some things he needs there, and I have come to ask if Mrs March will allow me to go with her. I shall be so glad if I can give her any help."

"How kind you are!" said Meg. "Mother will be very pleased, and we shall all be glad to know that she has someone to take care of her."

Everything was arranged by the time Laurie came back with a letter from Aunt March. It was not a very kind letter, but it enclosed the money for Mrs March's journey. Jo had not yet come back, and they were all beginning to wonder what had happened to her. At last she walked in, put twenty-five dollars into her mother's hands and said, "This money is for Father – to help him in his illness and to bring him home."

As she spoke she took off her hat, and they all cried out when they saw that her hair was cut short.

"Your hair! Your beautiful hair!"

"Oh, Jo, how could you?" cried Mrs March.

She seemed unable to say any more, but the look in her eyes made Jo feel that she had done the right thing.

Chapter 8
Illness

Breakfast was very early next morning.

"Children, I leave you to Hannah's care. And dear Mr Laurence will, I know, be a good friend to you. Go on with your work, and don't lose hope. Work is always a help in time of trouble."

"Yes, Mother."

"Meg, dear, look after your sisters. In any difficulty, ask Hannah or Mr Laurence. Jo, write to me often, and be my brave girl, always ready to help. Beth, your music will help you, and you have your little home duties. And Amy, I know that you will be good and try to help the others all you can."

"We will, Mother! We will!"

The carriage came, and they kissed their mother quietly, and tried to wave their hands happily as she drove away.

At that minute the sun came out, and Mrs March saw it shining on the girls standing at the gate with old Mr Laurence, the good Hannah and the friendly Laurie.

"How kind everyone is to us," she said, turning to Mr Brooke, who was sitting beside her in the carriage.

"Of course they are," he said, "because they all love you." Mrs March felt that the kindness of the young man would be a great help to her on her long journey.

When the carriage was out of sight, the girls came inside the house and they began to cry. Hannah wisely left them alone for a time. Then she came in with a coffee-pot, saying: "Now, my dears, remember what your mother said, and don't cry any more. Come and have a cup of coffee, and then we'll all work, as we promised your mother we would."

They sat round the table drinking the coffee, and Jo said, "Hope and keep busy – that's what we must do. I'll go to Aunt March as usual."

"I'll go to teach the King children," said Meg, wishing that she hadn't made her eyes so red. "But I'd much rather stay at home and attend to things here."

"No need of that," said Amy. "Beth and I can keep house perfectly well. Hannah will tell us what to do, and we'll have everything nice when you come home."

This made the girls laugh and they all felt better for it.

A few days later a letter came from their mother which made them all very happy. Although their father was still ill, he was getting better. After that, Mr Brooke wrote every day, and his letters became more and more hopeful as the weeks passed. Meg, as the head of the family, read these letters to the girls, and soon they were all writing letters to their father and mother and to Mr Brooke.

For a week the amount of goodness in the old house would have been enough to supply all the neighbours. But, when they knew that their father was getting better, the girls did not try quite so hard to be good.

Jo caught a bad cold because she forgot to keep her head covered up warmly after her hair was cut. Aunt March told her to stay at home until she was better, because she did not like to hear a person read with a cold in her head. Jo was glad to spend the time sitting by the fire and reading all the books she could find. Meg went every morning to teach the little King girls, but she spent most of her time at home in reading, again and again, the letters sent by Mr Brooke, and in writing to him and her mother. Amy forgot some of the housework she had promised to do, and she sat drawing when she ought to have been helping Hannah.

Only Beth kept on working. She did many of the things her sisters forgot, and she tried to help everyone. One day she said to Meg: "I wish you would go and see the Hummels. You know Mother told us not to forget them."

"I'm too tired to go this afternoon," replied Meg, who was resting in a chair by the fire.

"Can't you go, Jo?" asked Beth.

"Why don't you go yourself?" asked Meg.

"I *have* been to them every day," said Beth, "but the baby is ill, and I don't know what to do for him. Mrs Hummel goes away to work, and Lottchen takes care of him, but he gets worse and worse, and I think you or Hannah ought to go."

"I'll go tomorrow," said Meg.

"I would go today," said Jo, "but I want to finish my writing. Why don't you ask Hannah for something nice, Beth, and take it round? The air will do you good."

"I'm very tired," said Beth. "I did hope that one of you would go."

"Amy will be in soon and she will go for us."

"Well, I'll rest a little and wait for her."

So Beth sat in a big chair to rest, the others returned to their work, and the Hummels were forgotten.

About an hour later, when Hannah was sleeping by the kitchen fire, Beth quietly filled a basket with good things for the poor children. Then she put on her coat and hat and went out into the cold air, with a heavy head and a sad look in her eyes. It was late when she came back, and no one saw her go quietly upstairs and shut herself in her mother's room. Jo found her there half an hour later, sitting on the bed and looking very ill.

"What's the matter?" Jo cried, but Beth put out a hand as if to stop her sister from coming near.

"You've had scarlet fever, Jo, haven't you?" she asked.

"Yes, years ago, when Meg did. Why?"

"I'll tell you," said Beth; and then, beginning to cry, she went on: "Oh, Jo, the baby's dead!"

"What baby?"

"Mrs Hummel's. He died in my arms before she got home."

"Oh! My poor dear! I ought to have gone," said Jo, taking her sister in her arms as she sat down in her mother's big chair. "What did you do when the baby died?"

"I just sat and held him softly till Mrs Hummel came back with the doctor. He said the baby was dead, and then he looked at the two other children, and said that they had scarlet fever, and he told Mrs Hummel that she ought to have called him before. But she said, 'I'm so poor, and I tried to cure the baby myself, but now it's too late, and it's only with the help of others, Doctor, that I'll be able to pay you.' Then he smiled and was very kind, and he looked at me and he gave me some stuff to drink to stop me getting the fever."

"No, you won't get it!" cried Jo, holding her close. "Oh, Beth, if you are ill, I'll never forgive myself."

"Don't be afraid. I don't think I shall have it badly. I've taken the stuff, and I feel better," said Beth, trying to look as well as she could.

"If only Mother were at home!" said Jo. "I'll call Hannah. She knows about illness."

"Don't let Amy come in here. She hasn't had it, and I should hate to give it to her. Are you sure that you and

Beth fills a basket with good things for the Hummels

Meg can't have it again?"

"I don't think so, but I don't care if I do," said Jo, "because I allowed you to go to the Hummels in that way, when I was doing my writing at home."

When Hannah came she at once made them both feel happier. "Everyone has scarlet fever," she said, "and no one dies of it if they are treated properly." Jo believed her and she went up to call Meg. When they were together again, Hannah said, "Now I'll tell you what we'll do. We'll have Dr Bangs, just to look at you, dear, and to see that we start right. Then we'll send Amy off to Aunt March for a time, so that she won't catch the fever, and one of you girls can stay at home and help for a few days."

"I'll stay, because I'm the oldest," said Meg.

"No, *I'll* stay. If I had done my duty and gone to see the Hummels, Beth would not be ill," said Jo.

"Which will you have, Beth?" asked Hannah. "We don't need more than one."

"Jo, please," said Beth.

This settled the point, and Meg, feeling a little hurt, said, "I'll go and tell Amy."

Chapter 9
Life or death?

When Dr Bangs came he said that Beth had scarlet fever. He thought that she would have it lightly, but when he heard the story of the Hummels he looked serious. He said that Amy should go at once to Aunt March.

Beth soon became very ill. Dr Bangs came to see her often, but he was a very busy man and he was glad to leave Beth in the care of the good Hannah. Meg did not go to teach the King children because it was thought that she might take the fever to them. She stayed at home and did housework. When she wrote to Mrs March she felt that she ought to tell her mother about Beth's illness, but Hannah said, "No, my dear, don't say anything about it. Beth isn't so very bad, and it would be wrong to trouble your mother while your father is so ill."

Mrs March wrote from Washington that Mr March was not so well, and that he would not be coming home for a long time. Beth grew worse, and Jo, who attended to her day and night, was very troubled when she found that Beth did not know her, and that she called the others by the wrong names, and often cried out for her mother.

One morning, when Dr Bangs came, he looked at Beth for a long time, held one of her hot hands in both his own, and then said to Hannah: "If Mrs March *can* leave her husband, I think she should come."

Jo, who was standing near, turned white. "I'll send a telegram at once," she said. She hurried off and was soon back again. While she was taking off her coat, Laurie came in with a letter saying that Mr March was better. Jo read it thankfully, but the heavy weight did not seem lifted from her heart, and she looked so unhappy that Laurie asked quickly: "What is it? Is Beth worse?"

"I've sent for Mother," said Jo, with a sad look, as she tried to get off her heavy shoes.

"I'm so glad," said Laurie. He put her in a chair and pulled off her shoes for her and then asked, "Did you do it yourself, without asking anybody?"

"No, the doctor told us to."

"Oh, Jo, it's not so bad as that, is it?" cried Laurie.

"Yes, it is. She doesn't know us. She doesn't look like my Beth – and there's nobody to help us bear it."

As the tears streamed fast down poor Jo's face, she put out her hand in a helpless sort of way as if feeling in the dark. Laurie took it in his, saying as he did so – "I'm here, Jo. Hold on to me, dear!"

She could not speak, but she did "hold on", and holding the friendly hand seemed to help her.

At last she said, "You are a good doctor, Laurie, and such a good friend."

"I hope you'll get something tonight that will do you even more good," said Laurie. "I sent a telegram to your mother yesterday, and Brooke answered that she will be here tonight. Aren't you glad I did it?"

"Laurie, you're a dear! How shall I ever thank you? But what made you think of it?"

"Well, you see, I got rather troubled, and so did Grandfather. We thought that Hannah was wrong in saying that your mother must not be told about Beth – and we didn't like what we heard about Beth. We thought your mother ought to know. So we sent a telegram, and your mother is coming by the train which gets here at two o'clock. I shall go and bring her to you."

"Oh, Laurie, I'm so happy!" said Jo as he went away.

Jo went to tell Hannah and Meg the good news that Mr March was better, and that Mrs March was coming home.

Dr Bangs came, and after looking for some minutes at Beth, he said: "She is very near the time when there will be a quick change – either for better or worse. I'll come again later."

The girls never forgot that night. They had no sleep, for they kept watch in Beth's room.

Midnight came. Then another hour went by and nothing happened except that they heard Laurie starting for the station.

It was past two o'clock. Jo was standing at the window listening for the sound of the carriage. She heard a movement by the bed, and, turning quickly, saw Meg kneeling by the bedside. Hannah came to the bed, looked at Beth, felt her hands, and then cried, "The fever has turned. She's sleeping easily. And now she'll soon be better. Oh, how wonderful it is!"

Before the girls could believe that it was true, the doctor came. He was rather an ugly man, but they thought his face was quite beautiful when he said with a fatherly look at them, "Yes, my dears, I think the little girl will get better this time. Keep the house quiet; let her sleep, and when she wakes, give her ..."

What they were to give, they never heard, for they both went out into the dark hall and, holding each other close, wept tears of joy.

"If only Mother would come now!" said Jo.

"Listen!" cried Meg. "I think I hear the sound of the carriage."

The sounds came nearer. Then there was a ring at the door. Hannah opened it, and they heard a call from Laurie, "Girls, she's come! She's come!"

Chapter 10
The mother's return

Beth woke from a long sleep to find her mother looking down upon her. She was too weak to wonder at anything, but she returned the loving kiss her mother gave her, and then, without speaking, soon went to sleep again. While Mrs March sat at the bedside, holding Beth's hand, she told the others all her news.

Evening came. Meg was in the sitting room writing to her father to tell him of her mother's safe arrival. Jo went quietly to Beth's room where she found her mother in her usual place. Jo walked about the room, looking undecided and not very happy.

"What is the matter, dear?" asked Mrs March.

"I want to tell you something, Mother."

"About Meg?"

"How did you know? Yes, it's about her. It's a little thing, but it troubles me."

"Beth is asleep. Speak quietly and tell me."

Jo settled herself on the floor at her mother's feet.

"Last summer," she said, "Meg left a pair of gloves in the Laurences' house, and only one was returned. Laurie said to me: 'Mr Brooke has got it. He keeps it with his own gloves.'"

Jo looked up into her mother's face: "Now, aren't you sorry to hear this?"

"Do you think Meg cares for him?" asked Mrs March.

"I don't know anything about love and all that foolishness," cried Jo. "In stories, girls show it by getting red in the face and growing thin and acting foolishly. Meg doesn't do that."

"Then do you think that Meg does *not* care about John?"

"Who?" cried Jo.

"Mr Brooke. We began to call him John in Washington, and he likes it. He has been quite open about it. He told us that he loves Meg, but he wants to be able to give her a good home before he asks her to marry him. It must be some years before John can make a home for her. I hope that things will go well for her."

"Don't you wish that she would marry a rich man?" asked Jo. "I had planned to have her marry Laurie, and to have plenty of money all her life. Wouldn't that be nice? He's rich and kind and good, and he loves us all."

"Don't make plans for other people, Jo. Time and their own hearts will make your friends' marriages."

Chapter 11
A happy Christmas

After her mother's return, Beth got better every day. A small bed was put in the sitting room for her, and she was able to lie there during most of the day, enjoying the company of her mother and sisters.

The news from Washington was good. Mr March was getting better. John Brooke was still with him, and he wrote to say that they hoped to come home early in the New Year. So the March family were expecting a very happy Christmas, and with Laurie's help they made plans for having a great deal of fun.

"I am so happy," said Beth, "that, if only Father was here, I couldn't possibly be any happier."

"And so am I! – And so am I!" said the others.

Sometimes in this strange world, things happen just as they do in story-books; and it was so with the March family on this wonderful Christmas Day.

The girls and their mother were looking very happily at the Christmas presents they had given to one another. While they were doing this, Laurie opened the door and quietly put in his head.

"Here's another present for the March family," he said in a strange voice.

Then he opened the door wider, and a tall man appeared – so much covered up that his face could not be seen. Behind him was another tall man, who tried to say something but did not seem able to speak.

The first tall man uncovered his face and, with cries of delight, the girls saw that he was their father. It is not possible to tell of all that happened afterwards. The girls

Mr March comes home to his family on Christmas Day

and their mother put their arms round Mr March and kissed him. Quite by mistake, the second tall man – Mr Brooke – kissed Meg. Hannah came from the kitchen to join in the general happiness, and to tell them that the Christmas dinner would soon be ready.

Mrs March said to her husband, "Before we have dinner, you and Beth must have a little rest." She put each of them on a sofa, but Beth did not stay long on her own sofa. She joined her Father on his sofa, and they did not have as much rest as they ought to have done because they could not stop talking to one another.

Laurie and his grandfather and Mr Brooke all came to dinner, and it was a very happy party. After dinner the visitors went away. They knew that the March family would like to be alone together, and also that Beth and Mr March needed rest.

That evening the little family was gathered round the fire in the sitting room. Mr March was telling them how it happened that he came home earlier than they expected.

"When the weather became better," he said, "the doctor thought that I might come – and I wanted so much to surprise you all. I could not have done it without Brooke. He has been such a help on the journey – and, indeed, all through my illness, as your mother knows."

"Yes, indeed," said Mrs March, "he is a most kind and helpful young man."

There was a happy, far-away look in Meg's eyes. "Such a happy Christmas," she said, "and it has been such a happy year."

"How *can* you say that it was a 'happy year'?" said Jo. "There was Father's illness, and then Beth's illness – and all sorts of nasty things."

"I think that a lot of nice things have come to us this year," said Beth. "We've got to know Laurie and his grandfather, and I've played on the big piano next door, and I have a dear little piano of my own."

"And you went to the Hummels, and the baby died in your arms, and you got scarlet fever, and nearly died of it," said Jo.

"It was rather a hard road for you all to travel," said Mr March, "and the last part of it was certainly very hard, but, from all that your mother has told me, I know how well you have done, and I am proud of my little women."

Meg was sitting beside him. He took her hand in his, and he noticed that her fingers had become hard with needlework.

"Meg, my dear," he said, "I know how much work you have done to help your mother and sisters, and I am proud of this little hand. I hope that there will still be some time before I am asked to give it away." He smiled down upon her and pressed the hand which he wanted so much to keep near him. Meg tried to look as if she did not know what her father meant, but she did not do it very well, and she knew that Jo was looking at her rather sadly.

Beth whispered to her father, "Say something nice about Jo. She has tried so hard, and she has been so very kind to me."

"Although Jo's hair is so short," said Mr March, "she does not seem to be so like a boy as she was when I went away. I don't think she wants to be a boy any more. She is more careful about her dress, and she doesn't shout about the house as boys do. In fact she has become a nice quiet little woman! I rather miss my wild girl, but if I get in her place a strong, helpful, kind-hearted woman, I shall be very happy. I couldn't find anything beautiful enough to be

41

bought with the twenty-five dollars she sent me."

"And now what have you to say about Beth?" asked Amy. She badly wanted to hear what he would say about herself, but she was willing to wait.

"There is so little of her," said Mr March, "that I do not know what to say. She might easily hide away so that we could not see her. But I don't think she is quite so afraid of showing herself as she was." Then he remembered how nearly he had lost her. He held her close, and said with his face against hers, "I've got you safe, my Beth, and I mean to keep you now."

He looked down at Amy, who was sitting at his feet. He passed his fingers through her shining hair as he spoke: "I think Amy is rather tired, for she has been running about for her mother all afternoon. She wishes to be useful, and does not now think so much about being beautiful. That is a better way of making life beautiful, for herself and others."

Chapter 12
Meg, John Brooke and Aunt March

Mr and Mrs March often looked at Meg, as if they were thinking a great deal about her and the young man next door. They thought that something must happen soon. This state of uncertainty was not good for the little family, and Jo could see very plainly that it was not good for Meg.

Meg did not look very happy. It was clear that one of her dreams had not yet come true.

"What is the matter with us all?" Meg wondered.

"You know very well what is the matter," said Jo. "It is your John who is causing all this trouble."

"Don't say 'my John'. It isn't right and it isn't true," said Meg, but she spoke the words "my John" as if they were not entirely unpleasant to her. "I've told you I don't care much about him. We are just friends, and now that he is back again we shall all be as we were before."

"If he does ask you to marry him," said Jo, "what will you say? Will you tell him plainly that Father thinks you are too young, or will you go red, and begin to cry, and at last fall into his arms, just as people do in the story-books?"

"I'm not as weak and silly as you think," said Meg. "I know exactly what I am going to say."

"Would you mind telling me what you will say?" asked Jo.

"Well," said Meg, "*if* he speaks, I shall say, 'Thank you, Mr Brooke, it is very kind of you, but Father says that I am too young at present to think of such things, and I quite agree with him. So please do not say any more, but let us be friends, just as we used to be.'"

Meg had no sooner said this than they heard the front

door open, and a voice speaking in the hall.

It was the voice of John Brooke.

Meg and Jo both rose to their feet as the door of the sitting room opened.

"Good afternoon," John Brooke said. "I have come to ask about your father. I do hope he is not too tired after his long journey?"

"He is resting," said Jo, "but I am sure that he would like to see you. I'll go and tell him that you're here."

"Don't wake him if he's asleep," said John Brooke.

"I expect he's reading," said Jo, and she went away quickly, leaving Meg and John alone together.

As soon as Jo had gone, Meg also began to move towards the door.

"I am sure Mother would like to see you, Mr Brooke," she said. "Please sit down, and I'll go and call her."

John Brooke looked very hurt.

"Don't go, Meg," he said. "Are you afraid of me?"

He had never called her Meg before, and she was surprised to find how sweet it was to hear him say it. She wanted to appear friendly and easy, so she put out her hand and said: "How can I be afraid of you when you have been so kind to Father? I only wish I could thank you for it."

"Shall I tell you how you can thank me?" asked Mr Brooke. He was holding her small hand in his own, and looking down at her with so much love in his brown eyes that her heart began to beat very fast. She felt that she must run away, but also she wanted very much to stay and hear what she knew he was going to say.

"Meg, dear," he said, "I love you so much. Do you think that you can love me a little in return?"

Somewhere at the back of her mind Meg knew that this was the time for her to say to Mr Brooke exactly what she had told Jo that she meant to say. She knew also that, after speaking those words, she ought to bow to him, and walk quickly from the room. But her hand was still in his, and . . .

And the door opened and a new visitor appeared.

"Aunt March!" cried Meg. She could not have been more surprised if it had been a fairy or Father Christmas.

Aunt March stood in the doorway, looking first at Meg and then at the young man.

"What does this mean?" cried the old lady, striking the table with her stick.

"It's Father's friend," said Meg. "I'm so surprised to see you, Aunt March!"

"I can see you are surprised," said Aunt March, sitting down. John Brooke went out quietly, saying something about going to see Mr March.

"Who is he?" asked Aunt March. "Your father's friend. What friend?"

"Mr Brooke," said Meg. "The friend who was so kind to Father when he was ill. He went to Washington with Mother when the telegram came, and he stayed with Father all the time he was there, and brought him home on Christmas Day. I don't know what we should have done without him."

"Ah, now I remember," said Aunt March. "Are you in love with him?"

"Don't speak so loud," cried Meg. "He may hear. Shall I go and call Mother?"

"Not yet. I've something to say to you and I must say it at once. Now, tell me, do you mean to marry this young man? If you do, not one cent of my money will ever go to you. Remember that, and don't be a silly girl."

"I'm not afraid of being poor," cried Meg. "I've been very happy so far, and I know I shall be happy with him, because he loves me, and I . . ."

Meg stopped there, for just then she remembered that she had not made up her mind – that she had to tell "her John" to go away; and that perhaps he was quite near, and was hearing all that she and her aunt were saying.

There was something in the girl's happy face which made Aunt March feel that, although she herself was rich, she was a poor old woman living alone.

"Well, I will have nothing more to do with you," said Aunt March. "You are a very silly girl, and you have lost more than you think by what you have said to me. I came to see your father, but I don't feel that I want to see him now. I'm going home, and my last words to you are – I've done with you for ever. Don't expect any help from me when you are married to your Mr Brooke. Let his friends take care of you. You will get nothing from me."

Aunt March spoke so loud that she could be heard all over the house. She then went to her carriage, which was waiting for her in the street, and drove away in great anger.

When Meg was left alone she did not know whether to laugh or cry. She was not given much time in which to make up her mind, for the next minute John Brooke came in.

"Oh, Meg;" he said, "I couldn't help hearing – and I am so glad that I heard what you said to the old lady. How brave and good you were! And you *do* love me a little, Meg! You meant what you said?"

"I didn't know how much I loved you until Aunt March said those things," Meg began.

Aunt March finds Meg and John Brooke together

"And I needn't go away, but I can stay and be happy, may I, dear?"

Now here was another chance for Meg to speak the words which she had prepared so carefully – the words which she told Jo that she would say to Mr Brooke before bowing to him and walking from the room.

But she did not. Just as Jo expected, she said "Yes, John," and then she allowed John to take her in his arms and kiss her.

No one ever knew what happened in the sitting room that afternoon. Afterwards there was a great deal of talking, and Mr Brooke told them about his plans.

"I'm going to work very hard," he said. "I've got something to work for now, and I am sure that I shall make a lovely home for my dear Meg."

Mr and Mrs March already loved him as a son. They knew how good he was, and they allowed him to arrange everything exactly as he wanted.

Chapter 13
The end of the year

"Here comes Laurie," said Jo. She had been looking through the window, and had seen Laurie coming up the garden path with some lovely flowers in his hand.

When he entered the room, he went up to Meg, gave her the flowers and said, "For Mrs John Brooke." Then he offered his good wishes to them both.

"I knew you would get what you wanted," he said, turning to his teacher. "You always do. When you make up your mind to do a thing, it's done."

"It's very kind of you to say so," said John Brooke. "I thank you for your good wishes and I ask you now to come to my wedding, which I hope will be in the year after next."

"I'll come to it even if I'm at the end of the earth," said Laurie. "We'll both be there, won't we, Jo? But what's the matter?" he went on, more quietly. "You don't look too happy."

"It will never be the same again. I have lost my dearest friend," said Jo, who was almost crying.

"You've got *me* anyhow," Laurie answered. "I may not be much good, but I'll stand by you, Jo, all the days of my life."

Chapter 14
The little house

More than a year has passed since the evening described in the last chapter.

John Brooke was working very hard in an office and saving money. He hoped before long to be able to make a home for Meg. Meg looked prettier than ever. She had spent the time working as well as waiting, and learning to do many things which would be useful to her when she married.

Jo never went back to Aunt March. The old lady had grown to like Amy while Amy was with her at the time of Beth's illness, and she asked Amy to spend her mornings with her. In return, she promised that Amy should have drawing lessons in the afternoons from one of the best teachers in the town. This pleased Amy very much, and it pleased Jo too. Jo wished to give as much of her time as possible to writing. She wrote stories for the newspapers, and she was very pleased with the dollars that she was sometimes paid for them. Jo also spent much of her time with Beth, who had not been well since her illness. Although not really ill, Beth was never again as rosy and strong as she used to be. Yet she was always hopeful and happy, always busy with the quiet duties she loved, and she was everybody's friend.

Laurie went to college to please his grandfather, and he was having a happy time there. He made many friends. He was liked by everybody, and he often brought his friends home with him. When this happened, the girls of the March family were asked to meet them.

Amy was the one who most enjoyed this high honour.

She was very pretty. She thought so herself, and she was glad when the young men allowed her to see that they thought so too. Meg was thinking too much of her own John to think much of Laurie's young men. Beth had nothing to say to them, and she often wondered how Amy could be so brave as to talk to them as much as she did. Jo also talked to them, and it was clear that they all liked her very much, as she liked them.

Very soon John Brooke had enough money to buy a house for Meg. It was a very small house with a little garden. The garden did not look very good because it had only just been planted with seeds, but Meg saw it as it would be when the flowers were out. Most of the things in the little house were presents from her family and Laurie. Beth made the cloths for dusting and washing-up. Jo and Amy helped their mother to prepare the house for Meg and her husband. Aunt March sent a large number of very beautiful table-cloths and bed-clothes as a wedding present, but as she had said she would never give Meg anything, she pretended that the present was sent by a friend. Everyone laughed at the way she sent a present without breaking the promise she had made to herself when she was angry with Meg.

At last everything was ready. Meg and her mother went through the house together, and Mrs March said: "Do you like it, Meg? Does it seem like home, and do you think that you will be happy here?"

"Yes, Mother, I love it, and I know how much I ought to thank you all, but I am almost too happy to talk about it."

"If only she had a few servants!" said Amy who had just come into the sitting room after helping Hannah to arrange the kitchen.

"No, Amy," said Meg. "I don't need a servant. I mean to do the work myself, and there will only be just enough to keep me busy – as I wish to be."

"Sallie Moffat has four servants," said Amy.

"Well, she is a rich man's wife," replied Meg, "and she has a large house. In this house there is no room for servants, but I feel that John and I will be very happy here – perhaps much happier than Sallie and her husband in their large house."

Chapter 15
Growing up

The year which passed after Meg's marriage was a very happy one for the March family. Meg often came to see her father and mother, but towards the end of the year she became the mother of two babies – a boy and a girl. These children were greatly loved by their young aunts, and especially by Beth, who spent much of her time helping Meg to look after them.

Jo worked hard at her writing, and many of her stories appeared in the newspapers. Amy learned much from the lessons which were paid for by Aunt March. She could now draw very well. Another rich aunt – Aunt Carroll – was so pleased with Amy's work that she offered to take her to Europe. Mr and Mrs March were willing that she should go, and Amy looked forward with delight to seeing the pictures painted by the world's greatest artists – for she had already decided that she would be a great artist herself.

One evening, soon after Amy went away with Aunt Carroll, Mrs March and Jo were sitting together, and Mrs March said: "Jo, I want to talk to you about Beth. I am anxious about her."

"Why, Mother, what is the matter?" said Jo. "Beth has seemed unusually well since Meg's babies came."

"I'm sure that something is troubling her, and I want you to find out what it is."

"What makes you think so, Mother?"

"She often sits alone. She doesn't talk to me or her father as she used to do, and the other day I found her crying over Meg's babies. That isn't like our Beth. It troubles me."

"Have you asked her about it?"

"I have tried once or twice, but she looked so unhappy that I stopped. Dear Jo, you are so strong – and such a help," said Mrs March. "Now, you will try to find out what is troubling Beth, won't you?"

Jo promised, and for some days she watched Beth very carefully.

One afternoon she and Beth were sitting together. Jo was writing. Beth sat at the window with some needlework in her hands, but her fingers did not move, and soon the work dropped on the floor and Beth looked silently out of the window.

Then someone passed below, and a voice – it was Laurie's voice – called out, "I'm coming in tonight!"

Beth smiled and waved her hand as the quick footsteps died away. Then she said softly, as if speaking to herself, "How strong and well and happy he looks."

A thought came to Jo: "Beth is in love with Laurie! That is the reason for the unhappiness Mother has noticed in her. And Laurie kisses so many girls. He even wants to kiss me – which sometimes spoils our friendship. But I won't have it. He must love Beth, now that it is so plain that she is in love with him."

Jo lay awake for a long time that night. She was just dropping off to sleep when she thought she heard Beth crying. She went to Beth's bedside and asked: "What is it, dear Beth?"

"I thought you were asleep."

"Is it the old pain – the pain you had after you were ill – that is troubling you again?"

"No, it is a new one, but I can bear it," said Beth, trying to keep back her tears.

"Tell me about it. Perhaps I may be able to help."

"No one can help. But lie down here, dear Jo. I'll be quiet, and perhaps we can go to sleep together."

They were soon asleep, but Jo woke early and her thoughts moved very quickly. That morning she said to Mrs March, "Mother, I want to go away somewhere this winter for a change."

Mrs March looked up, surprised.

"But why, Jo? And where will you go?"

"I want something new. I feel restless, and I want to be seeing and doing and learning more than I am now. And I've got a plan. You remember that letter from your friend, Mrs Kirke, who has a hotel in New York. She asked if you knew anyone who would teach her children and give her some help in the house. I want to write to her and offer my services."

"Are these your only reasons for wishing to go away?" said Mrs March.

"No, Mother."

"May I know the others?"

Jo looked up and looked down and then said slowly, "Yes, Mother. I am afraid that Laurie is getting to like me too much."

"Then you don't care for him in the way in which it is clear that he is beginning to care for you?"

"No, Mother. I love the dear boy, as I always have – but not in the way he wishes."

"Have you spoken to Beth?" asked Mrs March.

"Yes. She would not tell me what her trouble was, but, Mother, I think I know it. I believe she is in love with Laurie."

"I had not thought of that," said Mrs March, "but it is clear that, for Laurie's sake, you had better go away for a time."

The matter was soon arranged. Mrs Kirke wrote that she would be delighted to have Jo in her hotel. Laurie came to say goodbye.

"It won't do a bit of good, Jo," he said. "My eye is on you; so mind what you do, or I'll come to New York and bring you home."

Chapter 16
Jo in New York

New York, November.
Dear Mother and Beth, – I'm going to write you long letters while I am here. I've a great deal to tell.

Mrs Kirke is so kind to me that I feel quite at home, even in this big house full of strange people. She gave me a funny little bed-sitting-room under the roof – all she had – but it is warm, and there is a nice table by a sunny window where I can sit and write when I am not teaching Mrs Kirke's little girls, or helping in the house.

I have my meals with the children, and I like this better than eating with all the other people in the house. My little girls are pretty children – I told them some stories and soon made friends with them.

On the first day I was here I saw something I liked. This house is very high, and it is a long way from the ground floor to the top. I saw a little servant-girl coming up with a heavy load of coal. Then I saw a gentleman who was coming up behind her. He took the coal from her hand, carried it to the top, and put it down at the door where it was wanted. Then he turned to the little servant, smiled kindly, and said: "It is better so. The little back is not strong enough for such a heavy load."

I thought he spoke like a German, and Mrs Kirke tells me that he is Mr Bhaer of Berlin. "He is always doing things like that," she said. "He is very learned and good, but very poor. He is taking care of two little boys, the sons of his sister who married an American and died here. He lives by teaching German and I am glad to let him use my sitting room for some of his lessons."

Mr Bhaer and Jo

Thursday

Yesterday was a quiet day. I spent it teaching my little girls – Kitty and Minnie – and writing in my own room. I was in the sitting room last evening when Mr Bhaer came in with some newspapers for Mrs Kirke. She wasn't there, but Minnie said to him very prettily, "This is Mother's friend, Miss March."

Kitty, her little sister, added, "Yes, and we like her very much. She tells us lovely stories."

Mr Bhaer and I both bowed and then we laughed.

"Ah yes, Mees March," he said. "I know that you tell them lovely stories. I hear them laugh. But sometimes I know that these little girls are not good. They do not work as they should – and that hurts you. Now, Mees March, when they are bad like that, you must call me, and I will come." He pretended to look very cross, like an angry schoolmaster, and the little girls laughed with delight.

I told him that I would certainly ask for his help when I needed it, and he went away.

It happened that I saw him again on the same day. When I passed his room, the door was open, and I saw that he was doing some needlework. I felt so sorry that he had no one to do this work for him, but he seemed quite happy, and did not mind my seeing him. He waved his needle at me and laughed.

"I am busy, you see, Mees March," he said.

Jo and Mr Bhaer soon became good friends. He gave her lessons in German, and he allowed her, in return, to do some of his needlework. It was a pleasant winter – and a long one, because Jo did not leave Mrs Kirke until June. When the time came for her to go, the children cried, and Mr Bhaer looked very sad.

Chapter 17
Jo and Laurie

Laurie worked very hard during his last year at college and he left it with high honours.

When the great day was over, he and Jo walked home together.

"You've done very well, Laurie," said Jo. "I'm proud of you. What are you going to do now?"

"That is for you to decide," said Laurie, in a voice which at once made Jo feel that the moment which she had feared, and which she had wished to put off as long as possible, had come at last.

"Jo," he said, "you must hear me. We've got to talk, and the sooner the better for both of us."

"Say what you like then," said Jo. "I'll listen."

"You must know what I'm going to say," he began. "I've loved you ever since I've known you, Jo. I couldn't help it; you've been so good to me. I've tried to show it, but you wouldn't let me. Now I must have an answer. I can't go on like this any longer."

"I wanted to save you this," said Jo. "I thought you understood ..."

"I know you did. But girls are so strange, you never know what they mean. They say 'No' when they mean 'Yes', and drive a man out of his mind just for the fun of it."

"Laurie, you know I'm not like that! You are very dear to me. You're the best friend I ever had, and now you've done so well at college, I'm very proud of you. But I can't love you in the way you want me to. I've tried, but I can't."

"Don't tell me you love that old German you were always writing about in your letters!"

Jo said, "Don't be so silly, Laurie. I'm not in the least in love with him, or with anybody. And he isn't old, but good and kind. After you, he's the best friend I have."

Laurie looked very sad. "What will happen to me?" he said.

"You'll love someone else, like a good boy, and forget all this trouble."

Jo told Mr Laurence the whole story of what had happened. The old gentleman was very kind. He found it difficult to understand that Jo did not love Laurie, but he knew that love cannot be forced, and he decided that Laurie must have a complete change.

He spoke to Laurie that evening. "My dear boy, I feel it almost as much as you do. I love Jo, and I hoped that she would become your wife – and my granddaughter. But the girl can't help it. I'm old enough to know that, and I also know that the only thing for you to do now is to go away for a time. Where will you go?"

"Anywhere. I don't care what happens to me!"

"Now, my boy, take it like a man. Most men go through this sort of thing once in their lives. Why not go to Europe, as you always meant to do when you left college?"

"But I didn't mean to go alone."

"I don't ask you to go alone. My business in London needs looking after. I'll want you with me in London for a short time, so that you can understand the business when it becomes yours, but I won't keep you there longer than is necessary. You can go to France, Germany, Switzerland, Italy – anywhere you like – and enjoy the pictures, the music and all the things that you've always cared about."

"Well, sir," said Laurie, "I can't say 'No' to your kindness. I'll come."

Chapter 18
Beth's secret

The letters that Jo had received in New York had said little about Beth's health, but when she came back, after being away for so long, she saw the difference at once. She knew that Beth was very ill. She had saved a little money in New York, and she asked her father and mother to allow her to take Beth to the seaside for a few weeks.

This gave great pleasure to Mr and Mrs March. They were glad that the two sisters should go away together, and they knew that Jo would take great care of Beth.

They went to a quiet place where there were not many people. They were drawn very close to one another by something of which, for some time, they did not speak – the knowledge that Beth had only a short time to live.

Jo felt quite sure that this was so, and she was glad when, one evening, Beth told her. They had been watching a beautiful sunset, and when at last the sun went down Beth spoke of death – her own death, which she knew must be quite near. For a minute Jo was silent and her eyes were dim. Then she said, "I've feared it, dear Beth, and for some time I've known it, but I'm glad you've told me."

"I've tried to tell you before," said Beth, "but I couldn't. I've known it a long time. At first it was hard to bear, and I was unhappy, but I'm not unhappy now, because I know it's best, indeed it is."

"Is this why you were so unhappy before I went away?" asked Jo.

"Yes, I gave up hoping then, but I didn't like to tell anybody."

"Oh, Beth, why didn't you tell me? You *must* get well."

"I want to, oh, so much! I try. But every day I lose a little strength, and I feel sure that I shall never get it back. It's like the sun going down, Jo. You can't stop it."

"It must be stopped," cried Jo. "You're only nineteen and I can't let you go. I'll work and pray and fight against it."

"Jo, dear, it's no good. Don't hope any more. Let us be happy together while we can. I don't have much pain. When we get home, Mother and Father won't need to be told that I shall not be with them very long, and they will need all the help that you can give them."

She was quite right. No words were needed when the two girls went home. Beth was tired after the short journey and she went at once to bed. When Jo came down she saw immediately that her father and mother knew the truth. There was no need for her to tell them Beth's secret.

Chapter 19
A meeting at Nice

While Beth lay dying, Amy was in Nice with Aunt Carroll, and Laurie was in London with his grandfather. For several months Laurie worked hard, but then he became restless, and Mr Laurence felt that he should go away.

"Laurie," he said, "when I asked you to come, I told you that I did not want to keep you here longer than was necessary. You've done well, my boy, and now it's time you had a change."

And so it happened that on the afternoon of Christmas Day, Laurie was walking in Nice. Laurie was lost in his own thoughts – not very happy thoughts – when he heard a voice that he knew – Amy's.

"Oh, Laurie, is it really you! Your grandfather told us that you would be here, but we thought that you would never come."

"I've been wandering about," said Laurie, with a rather tired and unhappy look. "Tell me, what news have you had from home?"

"Not very good news. Beth is very ill. I feel that I ought to go home, but they all say 'stay', so I stay."

"I am sure you are right," said Laurie. "You could do nothing at home, and they must all be glad to know that you are enjoying yourself here."

When Laurie went to Nice, he meant only to stay a week, but a month later he was still there. He was tired of being alone, and it was pleasant to be in a place where there was at least one person who came from "home". And Amy, too, was glad to see him, for they could talk together about the people and the places they both loved. Yet Amy was not happy about Laurie. She knew that he was wasting his time, and she felt that, if he was not careful, he would waste the rest of his life.

One day, when they were walking together along the shore, she said: "Laurie, when are you going back to your grandfather?"

"Tomorrow."

"You have told me that twenty times in the last month."

"Well, I have felt that I shouldn't be of much use to him if I went. I hate business, and I'm sure that I shall never be any good at it. In fact I doubt, now, whether I shall ever be any good at anything."

"But you did so well at college. You needn't give all your time to the business. I am sure your grandfather doesn't want that. What has happened to your music?"

"And what has happened to your art?" asked Laurie. "When you went to Rome, weren't you hoping to become a great artist? Don't you remember our dreams?"

"Oh, Laurie, when I had seen those pictures, how could I go on hoping then?"

"It seems then that we are the same, my dear. We are rather lost and don't know what to do with ourselves!"

They were now close to the door of Amy's hotel.

"What I told you was really true," said Laurie. "I'm going back to Grandfather tomorrow. I promise to learn something more about the business, and then I'll begin to think about my music, if you will promise me to think again about your art."

"Good boy," said Amy. "I'll do my best if you will do yours."

They shook hands, and in another minute he was gone. Amy thought, "How I shall miss him!"

Chapter 20
Laurie and Amy

Laurie went back to his grandfather, who was now in London, and he spent his days in the shipping office, finding the work much less unpleasant as he came to know more about it.

Soon after Laurie left Nice, Mrs Carroll and Amy travelled slowly towards Switzerland. They were at Vevey when Amy received the sad news of Beth's death. Laurie also heard it in London, and he decided that he would go at once to Vevey and give Amy what help he could. Jo had written that they still did not wish her to come home earlier than had been arranged.

Laurie knew Vevey well. He found Amy sitting in a pleasant old garden by the side of the lovely lake. When she saw him she jumped up and ran to him.

"Oh, Laurie, Laurie! I'm so glad you've come."

"I couldn't help coming," he said. "I only wish I could say something that would help you to bear the loss of dear little Beth."

"You needn't say anything. It is so good to have you here. Aunt Carroll is very kind, but *you* seem like one of the family. How long can you stay?"

"As long as you want me, dear."

Laurie stayed for a week, and each day he and Amy came to know each other better. On the day before Laurie was to leave, they were out on the lake together. Laurie was rowing, and Amy was enjoying the beauty all around her – the mountains, the cloudless blue sky, the bluer lake below and the boats that looked like white-winged birds.

Then her eyes met Laurie's. He had stopped rowing,

and he was looking at her so seriously that she felt that she must speak – as if to wake him from a dream.

"You must be tired," she said. "Rest a little, and let me row; it will do me good."

For a moment he seemed not to hear. Then, with a little start, he said: "I'm not tired; but you may row with me if you like. I must sit near you in the middle of the boat because I'm heavier than you are."

She took the seat that he offered to her, and they rowed together. Amy rowed well, though she used both hands and Laurie used only one. The boat moved easily through the blue water.

"How well we pull together!" said Amy.

"So well that I wish we might always pull together. Will you, Amy?"

For some time Amy made no reply. They went on pulling together. Then, as the boat touched the shore, Laurie asked his question again, and was answered very softly, "Yes, Laurie."

Amy and Laurie agree to pull together always

Chapter 21
Endings

For some time after Beth's death, Jo was very unhappy.
She missed the little sister to whom she had given so much
loving care, and with whom she had spent so many hours
of every day. She tried to fill her time by working for her
mother in the house, and by helping Meg with her babies.
She knew that Meg and John were very happy, and she
could see that Meg was both a happier and a better woman
because she was a wife and mother.

"It is plain that marriage has been good for her," she
thought. "I wonder whether it would be good for me. Or
am I – as I have so often thought – to be alone all my life?
Perhaps I'll just watch other people's lives, and put what I
see into books, instead of having a real life of my own."

When the news came that Amy and Laurie were to be
married, Mrs March was uncertain of the way in which Jo
would take it, and she allowed Jo to see this uncertainty.

"Oh, Mother," said Jo, "did you really think that I could
be so selfish and silly as to mind Laurie marrying Amy
when I wouldn't marry him myself?"

Jo found that the housework which she was doing for
her mother and for Meg was not enough to fill her life, and
she decided to go on with her writing.

Laurie and Amy were married at an American church in
Paris. Old Mr Laurence was so pleased that his grandson
was to be married to "one of the girls next door", that he
wished the marriage to take place soon – almost as much
as the young people themselves. Mr and Mrs March made
no difficulty, for they thought it right that Amy and Laurie

should be married while they were still in Europe, and spend a few weeks there before returning to America.

On the day that Mr Laurence and the young people were expected home, Mr and Mrs March went to the station to meet them and Jo stayed at home to help Hannah prepare a meal. Looking out of the front door, she saw Laurie hurrying up the garden path, as she had so often seen him in the old days. She ran to meet him.

"Laurie! My dear Laurie!" she cried.

"Dear Jo!"

Jo took the hand which Laurie held out to her, and they both knew that a strong and beautiful friendship had taken the place of their childish love for one another.

Soon the small sitting room was quite full. Amy came in first. "Where is she? Where is my dear old Jo?" she cried. Meg and John Brooke followed, each carrying one of their children. Then came old Mr Laurence with Mr and Mrs March. It was a very happy family party.

When the meal was over, the door bell rang and Jo answered it. It was Mr Bhaer. Jo was very pleased to see him.

Mr Bhaer had come from New York on business, and he often visited the March family. One day he told Jo that he had found work in another town and so he had to go away. Jo began to cry.

"Why are you crying?" he asked.

"Because you are going away."

"Jo," he said, "I have not riches and I have not youth; I have nothing but my love to give you."

She took his hands. "That is all I want," she said.

Questions

Questions on each chapter

1 1 What were the four girls' names?
2 Which of them was the eldest?
3 Which was the youngest?
4 Who received the girls' breakfast on Christmas Day?
5 Who sent supper to the March family?

2 1 What work did Meg usually do?
2 Where did Jo spend her days?
3 What was Beth's special love?
4 What did Amy want to be when she grew up?

3 1 Who was the boy in the passage?
2 What was the matter with Jo's dress?
3 What happened to Meg?
4 How did they return from the party?

4 1 Who went to see Laurie?
2 Who was Laurie's teacher?
3 Where was Jo when old Mr Laurence came in?
4 What surprised Laurie?

5 1 What did Beth want to do?
2 Why didn't she do it?
3 What present did Mr Laurence send to her?
4 How did she thank him?

6 1 Who dreamed of having a lovely house?
2 What did Jo want to become?
3 Why did Laurie decide not to go away?

7 1 Where was Mr March?
2 Why did Mrs March write a note to Aunt March?
3 What did Jo sell to get twenty-five dollars?

8 1 Who went to Washington with Mrs March?
  2 What news came in the first letter from Mrs March?
  3 Who visited the Hummels every day?

9 1 Two people sent telegrams to Mrs March. Who were they?
  2 Why did they send the telegrams?
  3 Who met Mrs March at the station?

10 1 Who kept one of Meg's gloves?
  2 Why did he do that?
  3 What was Jo's plan for Meg?

11 1 Why had Meg's fingers become hard?
  2 Who asked Mr March to say something nice about Jo?
  3 Who was "rather tired"? Why?

12 1 What was John Brooke doing when Aunt March came in?
  2 What help will Aunt March give to Meg?
  3 What did Aunt March's words make Meg realise?

13 1 What did Laurie bring?
  2 Who were they for?
  3 Why was Jo unhappy?

14 1 Who went to spend the mornings with Aunt March?
  2 What did Aunt March promise in return?
  3 What did Aunt March pretend?

15 1 Who took Amy to Europe?
  2 What did Jo think about Beth?
  3 So what did Jo decide to do?

16 1 How did the German help the little servant girl?
  2 What were the names of Jo's pupils?
  3 What did Jo do in return for German lessons?

17 1 What did Jo tell Mr Laurence?
  2 What did Mr Laurence decide?
  3 Where could Laurie go after London?

18 1 Where did Jo take Beth?
  2 What did Beth speak about at last?
  3 What did Mr and Mrs March know at once?

19 1 Where was Laurie on Christmas Day?
    2 How long did Laurie stay there?
    3 Why did Amy lose her hope of becoming a great artist?

20 1 Where was Amy when the news about Beth came?
    2 How long did Laurie stay there?
    3 Laurie wanted Amy to "pull together" with him always. What did he mean?

21 1 Which sister was left alone?
    2 Where were Laurie and Amy married?
    3 Who came to visit Jo?

Questions on the whole story

These are harder questions. Read the Introduction, and think hard about the questions before you answer them. Some of them ask for your opinion, and there is no fixed answer.

1 (a) Meg (b) Jo (c) Beth (d) Amy
Can you answer these questions about *each* of them?
1 What did she look like?
2 What were her special interests as a girl?
3 In what other ways was she different from the others?
Can you decide on the order of your liking for them? (That is, which do you like best, second, etc?) Can you give reasons?

2 What is your opinion of Laurie?

3 How does old Mr Laurence help the March family?

4 John Brooke: What opinion of him did (a) Mr and Mrs March, (b) Meg have? What is your opinion of his character?

5 What do you think of Aunt March? Was she as unkind as she seemed? (Can you give an example?)

6 Why is the book called "Little Women"?

7 Which of the girls may have been most like Louisa May Alcott? In what ways? (See the Introduction.)

8 What differences are there between the life of girls in the March family and the life of American girls today?

New words

college
    a place where one can study
    after leaving school

moment
    a very short space of time

scarlet fever
    an illness which causes red
    marks on the skin

shy
    afraid of company

skating
    moving on the ice on sharp
    pieces of steel fixed under
    one's feet

slippers
    soft shoes to wear in the
    house

sofa
    a comfortable seat for two
    or more people

telegram
    a message sent in signs (not
    spoken) by electricity along
    a wire